ALLOSAURUS

PTERANODON

CORYTHOSAURUS

APATOSAURUS

DIMETRODON

ANKYLOSAURUS

TRACHODON

TYRANNOSAURUS REX

STEGOSAURUS

TRICERATOPS

For my own little dinosaurs at bedtime:
Maddison Jane and Alison Isabelle
J. Y.

To Mom and Dad
M. T.

HarperCollins *Children's Books*

First published in hardback by Scholastic Inc., USA, in 2000
First published in paperback in Great Britain by Collins Picture Books in 2003

12

ISBN-13: 978-0-00-713728-2

Collins Picture Books is an imprint of the Children's Division, part of HarperCollins Publishers Ltd.
Text copyright © Jane Yolen 2000
Illustrations copyright © Mark Teague 2000

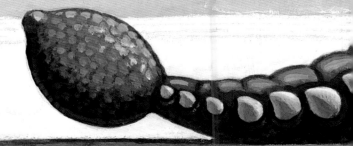

JANE YOLEN
How Do Dinosaurs Say Good Night?

Illustrated by
MARK TEAGUE

How does
a dinosaur say
good night
when Papa
comes in
to turn off
the light?

Does
a dinosaur
slam
his tail
and pout?

Does he throw
his teddy bear
all about?

Does a
dinosaur
stomp
his feet
on the floor

and shout:
"I want
to hear
one book
more!"?

DOES
A DINOSAUR
ROAR?

TRICERATOPS

How does a dinosaur say good night
when *Mama* comes in
to turn off the light?

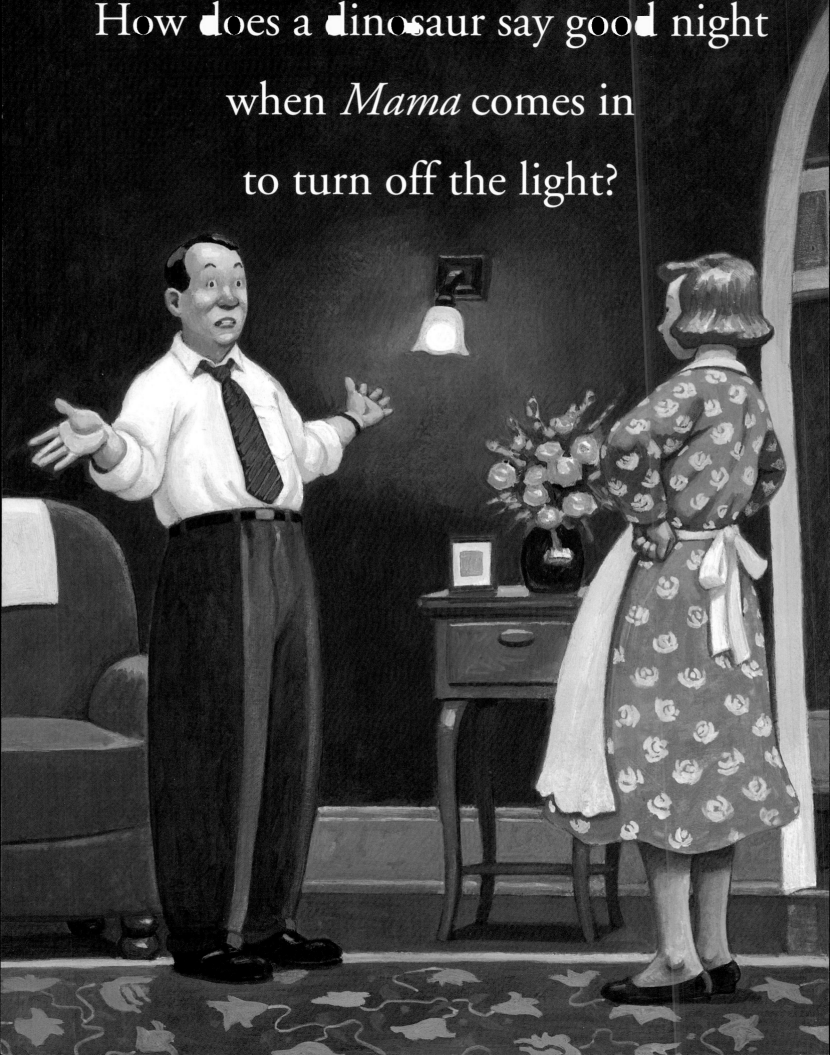

Does he swing his neck
from side to side?

Does he up
and demand
a piggyback ride?

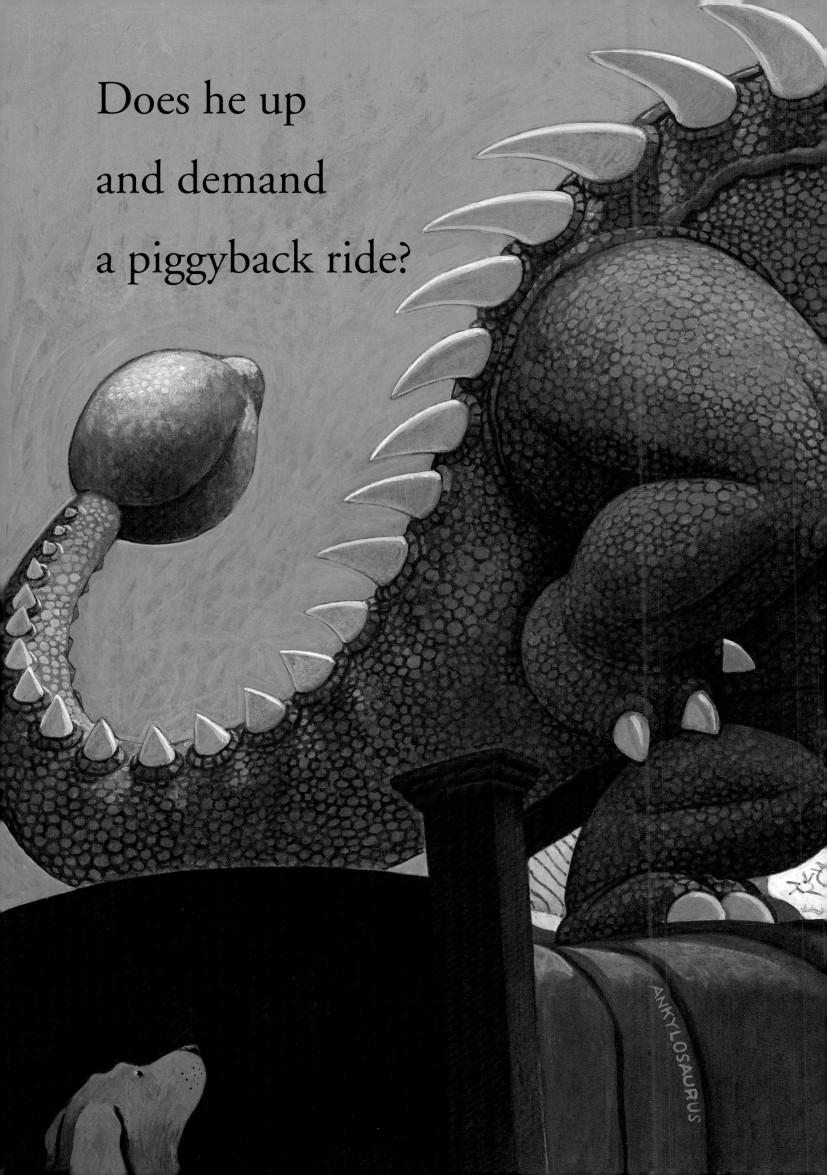

Does he mope,
does he moan,
does he sulk,
does he sigh?

Does he fall on the top
of his covers and cry?

No, dinosaurs don't.
They don't even try.

They give
a big kiss.

They turn out
the light.

DIMETRODON

They tuck in
their tails.
They whisper,
"Good night!"

They give
a big hug,
then give
one kiss
more.

Good night.

Good night, little dinosaur.